BITE

BITE
An Anthology of Flash Fiction

From the Editors of
TRACHODON Magazine
&
Cheek Teeth Blog

Trachodon Publishing • Saint Helens, Oregon

TRACHODON
PO Box 1468
Saint Helens, OR 97051
www.trachodon.org
www.cheekteethblog.com

Stories in this volume originally appeared on Cheek Teeth blog (www.cheekteethblog.com) between January 2010 and November 2012, except: "The Harvest Moon," James Claffey; "Back When We Knew Him," Rosie Forrest; "The Glacier," and "Epilogue," Jaydn DeWald; "Daddy's Here," Tom Hazuka; "Yellow," Lesley Alicia Tye; "Freezeout Road," Mary Emerick; "For Her Sixtieth Birthday in Cambridge, Massachusetts," Tara L. Masih; "Wipeout," Alex Mindt; "The Sex Lives of Other People," Ester Bloom; "Hercules Massis," Tom Weller; which appear in this volume for the first time.

Cover Photograph: "First of the Giants" by Anne Smith

ISBN-13: 978-0615721897
ISBN-10: 0615721893

Table of Contents

When I first pulled *Flash Fiction: 72 Very Short Stories,* edited by Tom Hazuka, Denise Thomas, and James Thomas, off the shelf in my father's library, and read the opening story, I knew immediately I could no longer be the same writer. That anthology, along with many other flash collections published since, simultaneously baffled and inspired me: How could these writers do so much with so little?

Years later, reading an anthology introduction written by Charles Baxter, I found an answer. Baxter explained that a novel can win readers over by points, but flash fiction has to win by TKO. Knock Out—that's what the best flash fiction does, marking a moment in the story with such vivid texture, the reader has no choice but to feel it right between the eyes.

Over time, my own style as a flash writer and editor has become refined. I'm a sucker for image-based metaphor and, perhaps against better judgment, I also love stacked adjectives. That said, knowing when to let a sentence run on, and when to cut something short, are also crucial to writing flash. A writer who employs a precise verb to conjure place, emotion, and action with a single word is a writer who understands about economy of language and allegiance to story. It's also a writer I'd include in an anthology such as this one, which is part of what I looked for when compiling flash fiction from Cheek Teeth to create *BITE*.

The worlds evoked in these very brief stories find their power in the details of life, not the tropes of high drama or violence. They rely on carefully crafted language and exact imagination. At just the right moment, they not only hit me between the eyes, but also in the heart.

~Katey Schultz
Celo, North Carolina

BITE

James Claffey

The Harvest Moon

We pull up outside the cottage the Old Man's rented for the fortnight. It's dark and owls hoot from nearby trees, "hoo-hoo-woo, hoo-hoo-woo." Across the road a frantic dog barks from behind a wire gate, and the Old Man shouts at me to help carry stuff into the cottage.

"I hope they control that bloody dog," the Old Man mutters.

The key is under a rock by the door, where the owner told the Old Man it'd be. When we go inside it's all dark and the corners of the room are spidery and shadowed.

"Sure, this is grand," the Old Man says, putting a suitcase on the ground with a thump. The roof-rack is filled with more suitcases and while Mam finds her way to the kitchen, we unload the rest of the luggage. As I'm going out the door the Old Man trips on a shoe scraper and falls towards me. I put my arms out to stop him, but he regains his balance, the sour smell of beer and whiskey hitting me in the face. "Jesus Christ, who put that bloody thing there?" He aims a kick at it and curses some more.

I cringe when he tries to kick it again. "Sorry, Da. I was trying to help," I say.

"Ah, don't mind me. I'm old and shook now." He fastens his coat and brings the next suitcase into the cottage.

Away over the sea, the reflected moon is a glazed orange ball. A harvest moon, Mam calls it. "Come and see the moon, Mam," I call out. When she comes out and we stand looking into the sky, even the Old Man admits it's a beautiful night.

"The glory of God," he says, a grin on his face.

"Will you come in for tea?" Mam asks, wiping her hands on the apron. "The sausages will be only good for dog food if you don't eat them soon." Inside, all the luggage put away, the cottage smells of rashers and sausages. Mam has the fire going already, briquettes of turf blaze in the hearth and the radio plays the evening Mart & Market report. Heifers are at a record price, and Leo Yellow Injectors are just the thing for mastitis.

When we sit down to tea the Old Man is licking his lips, the plate in front of him piled high with rashers, sausages, fried tomatoes, and toast. "Bless us Our Lord, and these thy gifts," he begins.

"Which of thy bounty, we are about to receive,"

BITE

I say.

"Through Christ, Our Lord," he adds.

"Amen." All three of us make the sign of the cross and the frenzy of knives and forks on plates fills the air.

Mam picks at her food, wincing every now and then from the baby's kicks. I smile over at her and she says, "Don't worry, everything is grand. Just indigestion." I know Mam doesn't want the baby to detract from our holidays, but she can't help it.

The Old Man reaches across and helps himself to what's left on her plate. A slice of bacon falls on his lap and stains his pants. "Shite," he says, picking the rasher off the floor and forking half a sausage into his mouth.

After tea I go out the back door and walk to the stone wall at the end of the field. Overhead, a galaxy of stars spreads out across the world. I imagine the time the Apollo rocket made its way to the moon—Aldrin, Armstrong, and Michael Collins heading for the lunar surface. For a long time I thought he was the same Michael Collins we read about in Irish History at school, but the Master smacked me on the head and told me not to be thick.

As the moon spins, the Old Man croons "Boulavogue" in the kitchen. Mam joins in as they sing, "For Father Murphy of the County Wexford weeps o'er the land like a mighty wave."

Across the water fog rolls in from the Atlantic and something rustles at the bottom of the field. Out of the gloom an owl flaps silently over my head, a small creature trapped in its claws.

Jakes' Games

If I don't flush I run the risk of the Old Man dragging me by the scruff of the neck to face the old brown trout and remove it by hand. There's only one toilet, outside the back door next to the coal shed. Mornings, the Old Man parks his arse in the counting house and reads the *Irish Press* cover to cover. Sometimes, I watch from the kitchen window for his business to be done, and a fair number of times the shite is almost leaking out of me waiting for him. He likes to linger in the cobwebbed jakes, cursing at the latest political news, and bemoaning those friends he knows in the obituaries.

When he sees me squirm from leg to leg with panic he calls me a baby and tries to block me from the jakes. This game pleases him no end, even when

I'm cranberry in the face and my eyes shrunken to pin-pricks. Mam smacks him with her apron string and warns him how he'll give me a complex.

The night I am trapped in the jakes when the coal-man dumps a bag of slack in front of the door is when he really gets it from Mam. They've been up the village for a drink and I am stuck inside the cobwebbed toilet praying for the light to go on in the kitchen. When I hear the Old Man's voice, he's shouting about some "Slip of a lipsticky bar girl with a lazy eye and an arse like the County Cork."

My cries go unheard, and it's only when the door opens from the kitchen and he comes out to get some coal that he hears my thumps. The Old Man heaves the sack from the door and when he sees me shivering in the dark he has a case of sneezing that brings him to his knees. He stands up and takes another look at me, laughs and points to my trousers, and says, "By God, there's egg on your chin, there."

My shirttail sticks out of my trousers and he keeps laughing and laughing, so I run inside and up the stairs to bed where for the rest of the night I draw cartoons of him drowning in the North Sea.

James Claffey *hails from County Westmeath, Ireland, and lives on an avocado ranch in Carpinteria, CA, with his wife, the writer and artist Maureen Foley, their daughter Maisie, and Australian cattle-dog Rua. His work appears in many places, including* The New Orleans Review, Connotation Press, The Drum Literary Magazine, *and* Gone Lawn.

Jim Shelly

The Bottom

By the time he made it to the middle of the lake with a slow, steady crawl, he imagined moss-green scales on his legs. Felt as if an easy flick of his pelvis would send him gliding down to where the sun seldom licked the bottom. There was something he needed down there— the languid ease of water, the drift and play of currents.

He'd worked all summer to get here, his muscles lean and poised. Holding on the sandy bottom for three and four minutes at a time, thoughts soaking out of his skull, he became wide-eyed to the shadows of rocks. When the gnawing need for air brought him back from fish, he'd push off and shoot to the surface, panting, floating till his heartbeat slowed, then go down again. And again.

The first changes he'd noticed were the tender red welts on his neck, running from his ears down to his collarbones. Now, he hung to a rock on the bottom, opened his mouth, and let the cold water pass through. He was trembling, lightheaded—but he knew. He knew that he could stay down longer. He put his fear aside and gulped again. Still okay. Still on the bottom with his fingers lightly locked in a crack in the rock, his legs swaying with the lake grass.

Jim Shelly *was born and raised on the east coast and moved west in 1975. He won the State of Vermont Frost Poetry Award and has been writing for 35 years. He is passionate about drumming, creative cooking, and how words can come alive in your hand. He now lives with his wife in the mountains of northeast Oregon.*

BITE

Tara Deal

Framework

Having trouble with my work, unable to create what the moment called for or to dislodge any new ideas from my floorboards, unhappy with my noisy neighbors whose fault it was that I couldn't get anything done, and failing, in fact, to make something of myself deep inside my flat, I went for a walk. As usual. Down one of my regular streets.

It was getting dark and blank and I almost did it. Killed myself, that is. That is, I almost stepped into the hole of an open basement—through the metal doors thrown open, flat on the sidewalk—one of my greatest fears. I wasn't looking where I was going, but then I did look down and, wow. It seems I had discovered something. Something awful, of course. There was blood on the floor. And frayed ropes. Pieces of duct tape had been yanked off something and now were stuck, fluttering, on the damp wall. I could even hear a struggle going on. Some sort of scraping. But I didn't scream, to my credit, nor did I walk away, which I probably should have. I did look around and over my shoulder. No one else there. A quiet neighborhood, unfortunately. Maybe even desolate.

And then, right beneath my face, out of the hole, a man came almost running up, with a wooden frame around his neck, smoking a cigarette. I froze, and he said hello, good evening, or something to that effect. Nice night for painting, isn't it? And I said, what? But then I composed myself and said I didn't realize what was going on.

No one ever does, the painter told me.

He came all the way out of the hole and put his broken frame on the curb, then stood against the bricks to smoke for a minute. I looked down and saw wooden benches with coffee cans of brushes and spatulas. And one large canvas, propped against the wall. A gray grid of stripes, with a yellow blob (a taxi, right?) and a dark odd streak, a pool of red.

The painter saw me looking in, studying his canvas. Maybe it was a work in progress. In any case, he threw away his cigarette. The agony of abstract art, he offered. And I said yes, as if I knew what he was talking about.

He closed the basement doors and I could hear a bolt.

Time to walk back to my room and try again. Because now I had an idea, if you know what I mean.

But by then, other artists had come out of their holes as well, and they slowed me down. They surrounded me with their shadows, bunched up under the wax-yellow streetlights, where they looked through the trash, picking up some things, hoping for a clue. Someone could use that bit of odd wood. The sky was turning, and soon it would be opalescent with a sheen of silver leaf. Another bright idea, and not too soon. But no, I couldn't count on that, the glow at the end of the road. And someone else had already grabbed the moon.

Tara Deal *is a writer and editor in New York City and the author of two books from small presses:* Wander Luster *is a poetry chapbook from Finishing Line Press, and* Palms Are Not Trees After All *is the winner of the 2007 Clay Reynolds Novella Prize from Texas Review Press. Her writings have appeared in magazines such as* Blip, failbetter, Fogged Clarity, Sugar House Review, *and* West Branch, *among others. And her shortest story can be found in* Hint Fiction *(Norton).*

Rosie Forrest

Back When We Knew Him

An old friend sat with us. It was the first time in a very long time and we shifted coolly on our stools. On stage, there was a band we all enjoyed. The bass player had a solo, and her instrument knocked her hip as she sang about a melancholy sailor.

Before he sat with us, he waved small and low, used the restroom, and stood some distance back upon his return. We all knew that wouldn't last. He's tall, this old friend of ours, so when he stood and stared at the backs of our heads, I felt as though the professor was watching. The professor, now isn't that a joke.

When he dragged a stool into the circle, two of us had to make room. We made just enough room and no more.

Our old friend didn't look well. His beard was untrimmed and his collar buckled under itself. A red plastic cup was half-filled with water, and he sipped his water through a straw, delicate sips that did not resemble the behavior of the friend we knew.

One by one we slipped from the circle and wandered outside for a breath of fresh air.

"The men's room is drowning in paper towels," Mike said. Mike was the newest member of the group and didn't know the extent of it all. He repeated his story as though we hadn't heard him. "Some asshole threw paper towels like playing cards all over the bathroom floor."

"Maybe there was water everywhere," I said.

I looked at the old friend, a look not tied to the bathroom incident, but it may have seemed accusatory.

No one mentioned the absence of his wife, someone we'd never met.

We checked our postures. We were slouching on our stools.

Conversation was difficult with this old friend. Questions were not directed at him, but he nodded as if they were. The high table made us feel like children; full drinks dribbled down the sides of glasses, darkening the black tablecloth with wet rings. In addition to him, there were six of us, and we paired off in quiet dialogue about the stubborn November leaves and a Midwestern football team that showed early promise. Our friend watched these conversations and nervously stalked the pauses for any opportunity to climb under our shared blanket of words.

BITE

There had been a time, not that long ago, when this friend held court. He had stories to tell and we circled around him, laughing big when the moment was right. As he told these stories (many about not giving a damn in this overwrought world), he swung a High Life by its neck, and when he took a drink, he swung the glass bottle high like a trumpet. We drank, too. Backyards and fire pits were littered with cans and cans of cheap beer from giant cardboard boxes, and we played guitar (well, one of us did), and we stayed up all night until a convention of birds pulled up the sun.

I should tell you my friend's name. He goes by Godric, a German family name he adopted because Rick was too forgettable, and Richard was an unremarkable name from the 80s. Godric enjoyed his singularity and created a number of idiosyncrasies to ensure he'd be remembered. He carries around a bag made of sheepskin, which resembles a shaved piglet clinging to his backside. He eats apples with authority and chucks the core into flowerbeds. He works by oil lamp and carves his own pencils. Or he did. Back when we knew him, he did these things.

"How's the store?" Godric asked. That's how we had met, working at Marjorie's Farmers Market, an organic grocery store, the kind with fresh pesto on display.

"Ellen's husband has cancer," I said. "Their daughter is helping out on weekends." I thought about mentioning the bad eggplants that arrived from Caster's the week before, how they were shrunken and shriveled when we opened the crate, and how the rotten stench made me sick, but that seemed excessive.

"What kind of cancer?" he asked.

"The dying kind," I said, and Godric didn't press me.

Two years earlier, our group had strolled late-night to Rye Beach. Our tongues and teeth were purple with wine, and we drifted back and forth across the sandy path. The wind was strong and I had wrapped a wool scarf around my face. Godric and a girl, a firecracker of a girl who resembles me in some light, stripped to their underthings and ran wild-limbed into the sea, the waves folding over their white, white bodies. They screamed, and we screamed back. She screamed, and again, us too.

It was a clear night but a dark one, and the mind played tricks. I thought I saw marionettes along the shore, wooden heads with rosy red cheeks, wooden legs that swiveled and kicked at the outgoing tide. They did such a dance, these hapless puppets.

Godric returned out of breath, his legs skinny and dripping. We watched the darkness for the girl. "Where is she?" we asked, and Godric, shivering, told us to help her, that he had gotten too cold, that with her weight on his back, they were both slipping under.

The girl was all right in the end. She cried a lot but mostly due to the sting of panic. "He let go," she said. "Like I was scrap metal." We covered her with our jackets and sweaters and scarves, huddled around her to make a warm nook. Far from us, Godric pulled on his jeans and stuffed half his white shirt in a back pocket. I saw him press his hands to his bearded face, and he held them there before drawing his fingers down his mouth and chin. He walked away then, and I thought I could see through him to the low hanging stars, this friend, this translucent stranger, I thought he might lift with the wind.

Sound Structure

It was an excellent tree house. Uncle Hurley from Frederick said so, and if Uncle Hurley said so, then it was, most definitely, excellent. Whenever Oliver lay on his stomach, he could see through the wooden slats to the place where the trunk split in two. At this hour, the sun had set, but the light dawdled; everything looked bluish.

"Statistically speaking, Oliver, twilight is the most hazardous time of day." That's what his dad said. Lately, his dad launched sentences with "Statistically speaking," and Oliver wondered what other kind of speaking there was.

But it was an excellent tree house. Sturdy 2x4s, the high-grade kind without knots, were the bones of the place, and real pine planks made the floor. The first official day in the tree house, four weeks ago or five, Oliver measured from each side with a 12" ruler and determined two points on the floor side-by-side. He marked them with a ballpoint pen and drew a circle around each dot. They looked like eyeballs. He sat there, on one of those points, on one eyeball but not the other, legs crossed, and spied a small spider repelling from the tree house roof. It was like Oliver was living inside the tree, like he had been swallowed by the oak itself and was part of something real.

The tree house was a sudden construction and was built in one weekend. It was July and the Maryland summer sky lobbed thunderstorms every day at 4pm. Oliver's dad slaved through the downpours, fearless amidst lightning and wind-bent trees. He was electric and hammered with an over-handed wail that made Oliver look away. Once, when the rain came, Oliver's dad, with tools in both fists, looked straight up and hung his mouth open. Inside at the large bay window, Oliver looked up at the kitchen ceiling and hung his mouth open, too, but he disliked how the stance tightened the muscles in his neck, how it choked his boy breath.

The tree house was an orange kind of red. Oliver had wanted it to be. His dad had suggested other colors like khaki and hay and moss, but Oliver said no thank you, those are "I'm sorry colors" and picked the least "I'm sorry color" he could find: Tomato Tornado.

When the tree house was finished and Oliver's dad had tested it for solid support and sound structure, he packed up his tools and tossed the black toolbox on an empty shelf in the garage, but he had not closed the toolbox latch tight, and the tools spilled down the back of the plastic shelving unit. There was a clanging of metal on metal that sounded like the crumpling of a guardrail.

"Statistically speaking, most car accidents occur within 5 miles from the driver's home," Oliver's dad said as they returned from the hardware store. One of the tree house floorboards had come loose and caused concern. Oliver's dad had shaken the board to show him saying, "See this? See this here? This is what danger looks like," but as hard as Oliver stared at the wood plank and his dad's thick hand pressing down till the fingertips went white, he couldn't detect a single movement in the board.

"Stay put and watch," said Oliver's dad. "See here. Watch this," his dad called out. The repair, Oliver couldn't see, but the pounding rattled his ribcage and pinched his teeth. "Watch how I make us safe."

The moon was bone in the daytime sky, and Oliver leaned his small body against the ladder, gripping tight the edge of a red rung. Blades of parched grass tickled his ankles, and he wanted lots of grape juice in a big white mug, but he didn't dare move because just overhead on that ladder, his dad, sweaty behind the knees, labored with wet rhythm, and the dull hit of hammer on wood, the blunt *one-two, one-two,* was the sound of his dad saving his life.

BITE

Rosie Forrest *holds her MFA from the University of New Hampshire, where she received the Thomas Williams Award for excellence in fiction writing. Her stories are published or forthcoming in* Whiskey Island Magazine, The Ampersand Review, *and* Prime Mincer. *Rosie teaches writing with UNH and Interlochen Summer Arts Camp.*

J. A. Tyler

Variations of a Brother War (Divisions Triptych)

There Are Equal Measurements

They do not make caskets for these soldiers. They make piles. They make mounds of dirt. They want to make open plots in the ground, but the freeze has sometimes hit and there is barely a war to keep lines with. There are two sides and on either a brother and in either brother a love for Eliza, who is in her cabin near her bed with the stove stoked and the rain outside her window threatening snow. But the prying open of Eliza's ribs takes precedence over this winter-air, over two brothers aiming rifles at one another's collapsing heads.

There is Water

The river in static motion. And there is never one place to set foot in. The voices that burble from it are fish or ghosts. And if they are ghosts then they are the ghosts of Eliza's father, the ghosts of Miller and Gideon's father, the ghosts of all the dead men from this warring. Or it is birds in the trees calling to other birds in other trees, trying to speak of how the river has and will always be and that the rain has the feel of winter in it, or how the ground is starting to seize.

There are Trees Holding Birds

And Miller and Gideon's mother, still living and alone in her cabin up the hill from Eliza, with the valley beneath them and the river bent towards their amputated hearts. A mother with her husband gone to ghost in war, with her sons, these brothers, both holding rifles up in the same war, on separate lines of the men, taking aim at trees or sky or their own boyish still heads. Eliza unable to speak with her, a mother knowing that a woman can only love two men at once if they are brothers, and if you are their mother.

J.A. Tyler *is the author of* A Man of Glass & All the Ways We Have Failed *from Fugue State Press, and* No One Told Me I Was Going to Disappear, *co-authored with John Dermot Woods, from Jaded Ibis Press. His work has appeared in* Black Warrior Review, Redivider, Diagram, New York Tyrant, *and others.*

BITE

Emily J. Lawrence

My Collection, 1995

Padagator was the name of the Pokémon my brother invented.

"Fans can send in cards they draw and they get to be real cards," he says.

We ride home from Wal-Mart in my stepmother's car. Water type: 90 HP. Attacks: Scratch (a classic) and Chlorine Eyes. Temporarily confuses opponent: 50 HP damage. Padagator is drawn on the back of an index card. I slip the trimmed card into the vacant tape cassette case I use to protect my holographics.

He flaps, "We'd get paid, too!"

He's asking me, do I want to? I check the rearview for my stepmother's eyes. "I guess," I say, kicking grocery sacks, a noise to guard my enthusiasm. My brother's tried to replicate each detail of a Pokémon card with his colored pencils. My stepsisters run fingers through their curls, lick their lipstick. I scratch the zit at the base of my scalp. "Are you sure they'll make it real?" I say. "Probably not," I say. Then, "Sure…I mean, if you're right that they'll really pay us."

My stepsisters collect, too, but they're the type who'd trade their holographic Raichu for a bag of Flamin' Hot Cheetos. We're the type who'd trade the Cheetos. We're a type; they're a type. I try not to be a type at all, but only hurt my brother in the confusion.

Years later my brother and I don't talk much. He drinks and tries to please everybody. When he can't, it's "Fuck all!" His enthusiasm has become cussing and tickling his girlfriend behind the closed door. I buy Pokémon Green, hidden in a box of Gameboy games, "$1 each, Buy Two Get One Free!" from the store where he works. He rings me up, chuckles, nostalgic. I choose you, I almost say. But that's dumb.

I'd like to say I still have the Padagator card, still pinned in the cassette case by the cross-shaped prongs, in my dresser or even fallen behind my bookcase, but I don't.

Emily J. Lawrence *is a bruised paper bag marked "Surprise" sitting in a dollar store. She broke into herself years ago and what she pulled out is what you read in her stories. These can be found in* A Capella Zoo, Hawk and Handsaw, Toasted Cheese, *and others. She is a reader for* A Cappella Zoo. *She is also founding editor of* Tremble Like That Review.

BITE

Greg Gerke

My Friend

My friend is sorry he hasn't been a good friend, but for a while his mind has been saying *fuck you* to everyone he meets. I agree he hasn't been a good friend and he gets more upset. You're to blame, he says. You make these behaviors happen. I want to comfort him as best I can, I want to hold his heart in my hand. Hold your own heart, he says.

I've only known this friend for a year and he has always been on my lesser friend list. His insults don't hurt me, but only make him more angry, like he is fighting with himself in my company. I want to go away but he is in so much trouble I have to stay. When he is this angry, his breathing is bad and his stomach hurts so much, he presses at it. This happens to me when I'm angry too, I say excitedly. Don't console me, he says, and don't talk about yourself. I don't want to hear it.

My friend can also be a kind man. He has a truck and helps people move things they normally couldn't, like couches, big tables, and bookcases. He never asks anyone for help, but will later complain after he has performed some tremendous feat with siding alone or when he removed a hornet's nest with one hand. That time he spoke to his worried mother on a cell phone and grabbed the nest without a protective glove because he lent his pair to someone who needed them more than he, but he soon realized this person often steals what is lent to them and those gloves cost a lot of money.

He sits in front of me holding his stomach and then talks about his father and how the old man would not be happy that his son is living alone and not too many people care about him. His father had all these friends and they drank and played cards three nights a week and now his son is considered cold-hearted because he wanted to charge a pregnant woman for helping her change a tire. But it was snowing and he had a slipped disk, he put his back on the line and actually his back hurt very badly after changing the tire and he missed work. It still hurts.

You don't really care about me, do you? he asks. Because I'm having a hard time in my life. I've been very unlucky and normal people don't want to be around other people like that, like me. So why don't you just exit my life and save me a headache?

He closes his eyes and sighs. Go, he says, but no, the voice is in my head. I do not move.

BITE

Greg Gerke *lives in Brooklyn. His work has or will ap-pear in* Quarterly West, Mississippi Review, *and* Gargoyle. There's Something Wrong With Sven, *a book of fiction, is available from Blaze Vox Books. He is the fiction editor at* ArtVoice.

Jaydn DeWald

The Glacier

Max came home late, wearing a gigantic fur coat and prattling on about a warm pool at the edge of a glacier. "Like sinking further and further into a woman," he said, winking. I told him he wouldn't mind eating a freezing supper then, would he, but he was already at the kitchen table shoveling my cold broccoli casserole into his mouth. When I poured his coffee, he chuckled and shook his head—told me he couldn't believe he'd actually seen the sun set over a polar castle, listening to Wagner, his pockets stuffed with little foil-wrapped chocolates. "Who knew your husband was such a swashbuckler?" he said and slurped his coffee. Later, sitting on the edge of the bed, I watched him take off a checkered sweater, flannel shirt, big black boots, three pairs of wool socks, and a thermal onesie. Then he began to describe—lurching stark naked across our bedroom—the "cut-glass ice" and "vaporous cold" and "almost feminine curves of windblown snow," etc. I cracked the biography of Margaret Thatcher I'd been neglecting. "Her father, Alfred Roberts, had been a Methodist . . ." Max stood at the foot of the bed, hands on his hips. Why wasn't I listening, he said, to his grand adventure? "I really ought to catch up on my reading," I told him, turning a page. I could feel him staring at me on the other side of the book, but I didn't let on. After a while he said: "You've become a real Iron Lady yourself, you know that?" Still later, in the middle of the night, I woke up hearing a faint sharp picking sound echoing through the house. I reached for Max across the bed, but he wasn't there. I stepped into my slippers, then started down the hallway in the dark. When I reached the kitchen, I stopped. The freezer door hung open, emitting a pale blue phosphorescent light, and I saw that Max had wormed himself deep inside the freezer—only his black boots stuck out—and was in there picking away at the ice. Quite suddenly, as if he could sense me watching, he looked up, then half turned his head over his right shoulder. That's when I saw how white it was, how it opened up onto a diamond glacier, row upon row of towering ice statues, a ghost-white path swerving into the distance, into the wind-slanted snow. "Max," I said. He stopped picking. "Wait," I said, and hurried back to our bedroom for a suitable coat.

BITE

Epilogue

If anybody asks what was his favorite part of her body, he will tell about an afternoon in Naples, on a white beach smudged with cloudshadow, when he woke to her lifting sardines out of a tin, slipping them whole into her mouth, and her ears—like curvaceous shells held to the light—glowed on either side of her head. In Amherst, in the mid-1980s, a flower vendor held the tip of a lit cigarette under the salmon-pink petal of a Cosmos, showing the poet Dara Wier how an emerald circle ("a little miracle," she said) will appear. And did her ears contain such miracles? Well, he once suckled a lobe in the dark-mirrored corridor of a dream hotel, his hands groping among the infinite, hissing layers of a crimson gown, and when he woke, orgasming in the dark, in their marriage bed, her left ear—a pale face, hidden behind the elegant Japanese brushstrokes of her hair—was watching him. As if they (her ears) had become aware of their allure, had begun in fact to tempt him, as when she practiced Yoga under a stone bridge in Winterset, wearing a lavender sports bra and black spandex shorts and fat turquoise earrings. Or as when, on their back porch, over iced coffee and pears, she had read to him a scene from Stephanie Vaughn's "Kid MacArthur": a student, a Vietnam vet, tries to give his professor a human ear from a bag of human ears. ("Can you believe that?" she'd said, and he, trying to disguise his morbid and inappropriate arousal, had mumbled, "Not while we eat, okay?") Perhaps then he will admit that her ears, once, in a nightmare, had rained down— slapping the truck beds, pocking the sea—that he, beneath a flowering lime tree, had wept for her, for all of her, the living body, her blinding white being.

An MFA candidate at Pacific University, **Jaydn DeWald** *currently lives with his wife in San Francisco, CA, where he writes and plays in the DeWald/Taylor Jazz Quintet. His work has appeared or is forthcoming* Aperçus Quarterly, New York Quarterly, West Branch, Witness, Zone 3, *and others.*

BITE

Tom Hazuka

That's All You Have to Do

Molly and her brother Pete were going fishing. She had never gone before. Usually Pete told her to get lost, because he was eleven and she was only eight, but Dad said Pete could use his fishing rod if he took her, and Molly would use Pete's. "Sweet," Pete said, because Dad's gear was a lot better than his. Besides, he told Molly as they walked down the road, "If you spaz and break my rod Dad will have to buy me a new one."

The pond was only fifteen minutes away. Molly was so excited she could barely stand it. She hoped people would see them and think she went with her brother to Porter's Pond all the time. She started to skip but forced herself to stop before Pete could turn around and make fun of her.

At the dam a short, scrawny man stood fishing with a long bamboo pole, no reel, line just tied at the end. His straggly gray hair jutted out from under a Ken's Kar Kare baseball cap that was so filthy Molly wasn't sure what color it used to be. They edged closer, Molly a step behind her brother.

The man turned his head and smiled at them. He had more wrinkles on his face than teeth in his mouth. Molly took a step back.

"Hi," Pete said.

The man tipped his cap with a hand that held a burning cigarette. Coughing, he pulled a small bluegill out of the water. With the cigarette dangling from his lips he unhooked the fish and tossed it in a dirty yellow bucket. The pail was half full of water, and a bunch of bluegills.

He baited his hook with a new squirming worm. Molly saw parts of tattoos through the holes in his T-shirt. Without rinsing his hands in the lake, he put the cigarette back between his fingers.

"What're you going to do with them, mister?" Pete asked.

"What do you think, boy? Fry 'em up."

"You eat bluegills?"

"Ain't no meat sweeter. And the price is right."

"Our dad uses them for fertilizer—plants them in the dirt with corn seeds like the Indians did."

The man swung out his line. "Everything's got a purpose on God's green earth."

"Goodbye, mister." With one hand in his pocket, Pete waved with the other.

BITE

The man nodded, exhaling a cloud of smoke. "Don't do anything I wouldn't do," he said.

Molly wanted to say goodbye too, but no words came out. She followed her brother. Down the road Pete showed her the red and white plastic bobber he'd stolen.

"But he was poor," Molly said.

"He had a bunch and we only had one. Now you have one too. Or would you rather give it back?"

Molly had no answer. They cut into the woods and climbed over a stone wall. Pete rolled over a rotten log and found some fat worms. "Come on," he said. "I know the best place."

She followed him a few hundred feet through the trees to a quiet cove. Pete put the bobber on her line but said she had to bait her own hook. "If you're too much of a baby I'll never take you fishing again."

The worm was slimy in her hand. Molly dropped the slithery thing twice before she felt the sharp hook pop through its skin, and it wriggled like mad. She wasn't sure how to cast, but didn't want to have to ask Pete.

Before she could try, though, he let out a whoop and started reeling. "Bluegill! Bigger than any that guy had."

The fish flopped at the end of his line. Grinning at Molly, Pete took a cherry bomb out of his pocket. He handed her a pack of matches.

"Light one," he said. "That's all you have to do."

He unhooked the fish. It gulped air, its eyes wide and staring. Pete popped the bomb in its mouth like a grape. He had to force it, but just a little. The water-proof wick stuck out like a cigarette.

"Come on, light it. Unless you don't want to go fishing anymore."

Molly's heart thumped against her ribs. "We're not supposed to play with matches."

Pete spat on a lily pad. "This isn't playing," he said.

Molly struck two match heads to shreds before the third one caught fire. Pete brought the bluegill to her trembling hand. The wick sizzled and he tenderly placed the fish in the water. Long seconds passed. Then a muffled explosion broke the surface ten feet off shore.

Pete laughed. "Cool, huh? I can't believe he got that far!"

"Cool," Molly said, her throat so tight she could barely talk.

Pete threw out another cast, halfway across the cove. He shook his head. "I can't believe that guy is low enough to eat bluegills."

Molly dropped the dead match in the water. A fish poked it twice before realizing it wasn't good to eat.

Molly turned away so Pete wouldn't see her wipe the tear off her cheek. Then she pressed the button on the Zebco 202 reel and carefully cast out the worm and the stained, stolen bobber.

"Pretty darn good for your first try, Moll," Pete said, and though her stomach felt full of worms his little sister couldn't help smiling.

BITE

Daddy's Here

I'm supposed to pick up my son at three. I get there half an hour early.

"Daddy's here!" Jim calls through the screen door.

"I thought you said three," my ex-wife says.

"What? Am I late?"

Beth rolls her eyes. "Go someplace close," she says. "Get him home for supper, okay?"

"We'll have fish," Jim says. "I'll catch 'em."

"Actually, we'll throw them back if we get any. I know how much your Mom likes to clean fish."

Beth nods. "It's right up there with toothpicks under the fingernails. Give me a kiss."

I do, a quick one on the mouth. She's caught so off guard she blushes, something I've rarely seen.

"Oh, you meant Jim?" I say, and feel the heat in my own cheeks.

"You're funny, Daddy," Jim says.

"Get out of here, both of you," Beth says, sounding scarily like my mother.

I put my son's gear next to mine in the back seat. We drive three miles to Keller's Pond and park on the side of the road. A short walk through the woods there's a shallow cove I know about, with a submerged stone wall thirty feet off shore. What was this place when the wall was on dry land, when someone had spent months creating it? Fish congregate around the wall, and Jim's in no danger of getting hung up. He's only six years old and probably can't cast that far anyway.

The ground is damp from the rain, even in the woods. We turn over a rotten log and a few rocks, and in five minutes have more than enough bait.

"Want me to put the worm on your hook?"

"I know how."

He doesn't, not really, but after a few tries and a lot of squirming the worm ends up skewered. It doesn't matter; sunfish will hit anything. I clip on a plastic bobber two feet from the hook. The first cast goes backward, and the second, and I have some untangling to do in the bushes. Finally he gets a decent one out there, ten feet or so.

"Beautiful, Jimbo!" I say, and my boy tries to pretend he's not proud of himself.

The red and white bobber sits motionless on the skin of the pond. We watch it like campers around a fire, as if a secret waits inside. Suddenly it wiggles, just barely, so little at first that any kid's imagination could do better. But then it starts dancing. My son's eyes come alive.

"Now!" I say.

The fish hooks itself. I see Jim's clenched teeth as he reels. His cheap little pole bows hard toward the water, and for a weak moment I almost reach to help him. But I resist the impulse and leave him alone.

A bluegill flops in the air at the end of the line, twisting, fighting to throw the hook. Jim keeps cranking though the bobber is already jammed up against the rod tip. The drag screeches.

"You got him," I say. "Stop reeling." He does, watching the fish struggle.

Amazement a pulse away from fear shines in his face.

"Do you want me to take him off the hook?"

He shakes his head.

"Do you want to?"

He swallows and doesn't answer.

"Grab him on the belly. He won't hurt you."

He reaches but the fish jumps and his hand shoots back. Again and again he tries but the bluegill has plenty of life left, plenty of fear to keep him thrashing.

"Let me do it for you."

My son won't look at me. He drops the pole and lays the fish on the shore where it bucks madly, coating itself with dirt, rubbing off its protective slime. Jim pins it to the ground with his sneaker. He squats and works. The hook is deep, too deep for me to see. When he finishes, he lifts his foot. The fish doesn't move.

My son squints at his bloody hook. I prepare to comfort him, to tell him these things happen boy but your Daddy's here, it'll be all right.

"Jerk ate my worm," he says, and reaches in the coffee can for another one.

Tom Hazuka *has published three novels,* The Road to the Island, In the City of the Disappeared, *and* Last Chance for First, *and co-edited four anthologies of short stories:* Flash Fiction; Sudden Flash Youth; You Have Time for This; *and* A Celestial Omnibus: Short Fiction on Faith. *He teaches fiction writing at Central Connecticut State University.*

BITE

Jenny Robertson

Cry Room

"You really want to eat that?" David, my husband, says to Corey, who is stuffing ancient alphabet blocks into his mouth. Corey smiles without teeth at his father and goes back to toughening his gums on germy wood.

"*Sara.*" David turns to me.

His eyes plead like those of the stained glass Jesus that looks down on us from the back wall of Prince of Peace Lutheran, my mother's church. On this Sunday of our visit, when we are supposed to sit together as a family, the three of us have left my mother alone out in the pews.

"I know," I say, and squeeze his shoulder.

This Sunday ritual is not one David and I usually perform. We don't brag about our child's ability to sit through novenas and never-ending prayers, not about his angelic cheeks or curls—although he has them.

My son saw the old ladies coming for him, leaning in from all sides of the church, reaching for him all perfume and talcum, and he screamed. My mother, who says all babies adore her, looked at me with eyes that said without words—you have ruined this for me—and frowned even more deeply when her cherub Corey turned into a bucking giant whoopy cushion, bright red and gushing tears and noises. She pushed him back to me and we skulked down the aisle to the closed-off cry room where we are pariahs, unseen and unheard, but still expected to watch and listen.

Suffer the little children, Jesus said, but the church women won't have it: children noisy, children refusing to sleep cozy on their bosoms, children not behaving like the angels their grandmothers tell the other grandmothers they are. I don't mind our banishment—this is not my congregation—I don't even mind my mother's frustration. We're here with her, which is what she wanted. And we're frustrating her, which is something I seem to have worked at my whole life.

"We're irredeemable," I say to David, and nudge him to look at his son, who is now on his hands and knees on the cry room carpet, chewing a valley into the binding of a book.

"At least it's not a Bible." David says. He mimes gnawing on a tall stack of psalms and edicts.

Above the pastor's head, stained glass Jesus glows golden with sun. His arms reach out to the lambs at his feet. Beneath Him, the ladies of Prince of Peace kneel to take their wafers and wine and all the many blessings of communion.

Jenny Robertson *is a poet, painter, and fiction writer living near Traverse City, Michigan. Her poems have appeared in* Dunes Review *and* Greatest Lakes Review, *and she was the 2012 recipient of the William J. Shaw Memorial Prize for Poetry. Her chapbook of short stories,* Hard Winter, First Thaw, *was published in 2009. She is currently enrolled in the Pacific University MFA in Writing program.*

Damon McLaughlin

A Certain Slant of Light

Layla, with the warm sun at her back, focused on the small white circle inside her cardboard box projector. A perfect, dark bite had been taken from its upper-right corner. If the moon had progressed further through the eclipse in this last second, last minute, hour, such progress remained unremarkable.

"Lemmee see, lemmee see," Maia chanted, tugging at the underside of the box. "Mom, lemmee see."

Layla shifted the box over the head of her daughter. She tipped it until, on the distant end, an incomplete sun wavered on the white paper they had taped there.

"See it?"

"That's it?"

"That's it. Nothing's changed."

For what else could Layla say? She hadn't found peace like that since college when, having given the *Upanishads* a cursory read at best, the universe spilled open like a saguaro's white bloom and as quickly wilted. She recalled this much. But moments ago, she had been back in college. She had been on the front porch of her girlfriend's house with Happold's *Mysticism* opened spine-down on her lap. On the sidewalk with the box, with her daughter, she maintained the sensation of having returned *somewhere* just now, but the recall of who-what-where-when-why escaped her. The feel of the book in her hands, the book, the couch, the overcast winter sky that day—it had all fallen into the rift, and the rift had closed.

"I don't see it," Maia complained, her head blocking the pinhole-sized slant of sunlight that streamed through the projector. "You're not holding it right."

"Woops. Sorry."

Layla maneuvered the box until the deformed white circle reappeared. Everything, she thought, was like this: enchanting, transient, out of reach the moment her hands held it. Wherever she had been just now—through and back through whatever hole had appeared—only an imprisoned, unnamable splendor remained.

Maia raised an eyebrow. "What's the big deal again? When did this happen before?"

"Just watch," Layla said, ignoring any further questioning, tugging Maia down to her side. So what if the sun was being imperceptibly slowly hollowed out by the moon? "Sit down," she said. "You'll see."

BITE

Damon McLaughlin *is a poet and musician from Tucson, Arizona. His chapbook* Olduvai Theory *won the 2011 Toad Hall Press Chapbook Contest;* Exchanging Lives *(Backwaters Press, 2008) is his first full-length collection. He blogs at "Present Everywhere, Visible Nowhere."*

Jenean McBrearty

Fear of the Dark

Another blast and the shelter went black. Edie heard a man next to her say, "Bloody bastards," but nobody screamed or prayed this time. At least out loud. Maybe because there were no children in the shelter tonight. Unfortunate. Edie counted twelve explosions that might have hit twelve houses where children cowered in cellars with parents who struggled to get their gas masks on properly. If they could find them in the dark.

"If this was New York instead of London, the Americans would be in this war alright," the same man said. Edie caught the same whiff of whiskey as he spoke.

"If they was bombing New York, we'd all be spreckin the dough-chee," a woman said and laughter rippled through the tube. She sounded like Maude, pub keeper extraordinaire who never watered down the beer.

The night chill was wearing off, a stale, humid human stuffiness taking its place. "Stay put," a defense captain yelled down at them through his mask, "lots of smoke up here. Can't see a thing." The all-clear siren blew, but nobody moved. Edie felt a hand grope for hers.

"Congratulations, we made it through another night," the man said. She shook his hand.

"Nice to meet a fellow survivor," she said but when she pulled her hand away, he held it a little tighter. She was transported to her grandfather's bedside, holding his hand as death approached.

She let her pocketbook slide down her other arm and patted his hand with her free hand. Someone started singing *God Save the King,* and muffled voices chimed in. It wasn't the first time people had carried pub camaraderie into a shelter. They'd have a song fest now. Were other people holding hands? It was too dark to tell.

The man moved her hand slowly to his leg. It was tight and muscular. She could feel his pulse beating as he pulled it towards his inner thigh, then up to the bulge in his crotch. She waited for the sound of a zipper, but felt buttons. He was a sailor. She hadn't noticed any sailors in the pub, but by nine o'clock, she was on her second pint, and mad as hell Ian left with a blonde floozy. Hopefully they made it to a shelter.

The man worked three buttons open and she felt a fat taut piece of flesh caressing her hand. He covered her hand with his and clasped it around the stalwart

BITE

sailor standing at attention. It was outrageous, but all wars are. Her father told her stories of the French women in the last one, doing what they had to do to cope with the death notices they received by the thousands. England was lucky. No trenches on her soil.

The man was breathing in hard halting bursts, unnoticed in the gusty refrains of a First World War favorite. *Over There*. He would tell his buddies about this some night, maybe be right in the middle of the story when a U-boat fired a torpedo and blew a hole in the lower deck.

She heard gasps turn into slow, heavy breaths and wiped her hand on his under-shirt. She'd tell her girlfriends about this someday, maybe she'd be right in the middle of the story when the postman brought her a death notice about Ian.

Each passing minute might be the last for them. Each breath a desperate plea that the target of the bomb, the bullet, the death bulletin would always be for someone else—a stranger one had never touched.

She held her mask in her hands, and her tears flowed. She felt her shoulders sob in small jerks. An arm came round her shoulder and a head pressed next to hers. She was wrong. Neither of them would ever speak of being afraid and making love in the dark.

Jenean McBrearty *is a graduate of San Diego State University and taught Political Science and Sociology at Des Moines Area Community College. She received the EKU English Department's Award for Graduate Non-fiction (2011), and has been published in* Main Street Rag Anthology—Altered States, Wherever It Pleases, Danse Macabre, bioStories, Cobalt Review, *and* Black Lantern, *among others.*

BITE

Brendan Isaac Jones

Mitch

When I was nine I netted a small fish in the Loyalsock River. I put him in a bucket and called him Mitch. My father let me keep my fish, but by the time we got back to Philadelphia, my new pet was dead.

Not ready to let go, I put Mitch into a Ziploc bag and stuck him in the icebox. Each afternoon when I arrived home from school, I made a beeline for the kitchen and took Mitch out for a swim. I filled the bathtub and sailed him around him in great swoops. SHWEEEOO! At a certain point, Mitch thawed and softened, and I was forced to return him to the freezer for a couple hours before he was ready to go again.

This went on for four years.

In one family picture, my sister rubs her cheek

against Moses, our cat, my father holds the collar of Pete, our chocolate Lab, and I hold Mitch out proudly in an open palm. There he sits, staring out of his Ziploc bag, his silver scales reflecting the white of the flash.

At 13, the two small indentations on either side of Mitch's body where I put my fingers began to meet one another. Most of his scales had flaked away and he had become sand-colored. That winter, following a terrific argument with my father, I buried my fish in the frozen ground. I found a stone and scrawled in chalk: *Here lies Mitch, dear fish, August 19, 1985 - January 4, 1989.*

Dead or alive, I loved that fish. His life was measured not by heartbeats, but by how long he was able to swim in my hand.

Born in Colorado, **Brendan Isaac Jones** *was raised in Philadelphia. In 1997 he moved to Alaska, where he worked on fishing boats. He received a B.A. and M.A. from Oxford University. He has been a resident at the MacDowell Colony, has published work in* Narrative Magazine, *and recorded pieces for NPR. He lives in Sitka, Alaska where he is finishing his first novel,* The Bell Ringer.

BITE

Charles Heiner

Before

Those kindergarten weekends, you and Kate walked with your mothers to the churchyard fair, up the dead-end street, the long hill, slowly moving closer to the sun that filtered through the trees. The fair was dull. You saw the clown, or looked at the orange goldfish they sold in plastic bags. But Kate was there. She had bows in her hair, and wore that ruffled, red plaid dress. Afterwards, while tea was served in her mother's living room, she'd sit across from you on the floor and pull up her knees so high that you could see her underwear. You'd stare at her from your soft chair and barely say a word. She'd grow restless. She'd huff and pout. She'd turn to her mother and loudly ask when you were going home.

Before you left her for a different school in the fifth grade, played JV soccer, studied plate tectonics, ignored the flirtations of pretty girls you were afraid to talk to, stared at their tight jeans, and heard one morning before class of how her parents found her body, hanging from the clothes rack, cold, her bathrobe belt wrapped tight around her neck, you wanted to get off your chair and go sit down by her side, closer to the warm, wet sound of her breath.

Charles Heiner *has an MFA in Creative Writing from McNeese State University. His writing has appeared in* The Laurel Review, Fiction Weekly, *and* Dirtflask. *One of his short stories was shortlisted for the Faulkner-Wisdom Creative Writing Competition. He lives in Charlottesville, Virginia.*

BITE

Lesley Alicia Tye

Yellow

She stood in front of the lilac bush, listening to the sound of metal grating metal as she opened and closed the shears in her hand. Up until this year, spring had always been her favorite season. It was a cliché, sure, but she loved watching the world renew life all around her. In particular, she marveled at the way the landscaping they'd planted their first year in the house not only found its way back to green even after the harshest winter, but how it grew in size and scope each new spring.

It wasn't until the third year that the dwarf lilac bushes even blossomed, the tiny buds giving off a fragrance strong enough to smell indoors when the windows were left open. The butterflies went crazy for those lilacs. Orange Monarchs sailed from one clump of flowers to another and tiny Skippers darted alongside the bumblebees. The Eastern Tiger Swallowtails were her favorite, with their yellow and black stripes and blue spots along the bottom.

Every afternoon she stood outside to watch them. It was incredible how many there were. She stood close enough to touch the soft tuft of their bodies, filling a whole memory card full of pictures of butterflies that spring. James had several framed as a gift that winter, soon after she shared the news. "For our own little pupa," he'd said to her, and the nickname stuck. Had it really been coincidence that the yellow paint they'd picked from the swatches was named Butterfly Bush? Everything seemed to be butterflies. Even the small stain on the mattress she found weeks after her return from the hospital looked like rusty wings spreading across the fabric.

"You love the spring," James had reminded her that morning, since she was actually up and moving around before he left for the office. "You should take a walk. Get out of the house." He reached out to touch her and she veered away toward the coffee pot, pretending to refresh her cup. It wasn't fair. James had lost something, too. But how could she tell him that every time he tried to reach her, even through words, the numbness gave way to an ache that started at the center and radiated through every vein?

Once he left, she resolved to try his suggestion, shedding the bathrobe like a second skin. She went through the garage, sunlight washing over her toes as

BITE

the noisy automatic door opened. She was about to step out when the glint of the silver shears hanging alongside the abandoned garden tools caught her eye. She'd read up carefully on the care of her lilacs when they were first planted, how they were to be clipped immediately after they were done blooming, only after the flowers had died off. That was the way to ensure new buds in the spring.

As she walked around to the front of the house the scent of the lilacs hit her suddenly. She doubled over, remembering the sensation of sickness, but nothing came. After a moment she straightened back up. The bushes were slightly taller now, the butterflies doubled in number. She tried to name them: Swallowtails, Longwings, True Brushfoots. Watching them now she could only think of the shell of their empty cocoons, abandoned and useless.

She hadn't even remembered picking up the shears, but they were in her hand now. What would James say when he came home to find the bushes clipped clean of all their flowers? She didn't care. She watched the way the sunlight played across the metal blades, opening and shutting like wings.

Green

Because that was the summer you found the frogs. It had been magical. The kids squealing as they chased fingernail-sized jumpers all around the back yard. You took them to the library and checked out reptile books to help with identification. Scoured the Internet for sites on how to make your backyard into a haven for wildlife. Spent the vacation money on materials to create a backyard pond, with the wife's permission, of course. Suddenly that little plot of grass became a fairyland.

But there had to be a casualty. You thought for sure the culprit would be the dog, but it was actually you. One wrong step and Jessica screamed--you squashed that frog so flat, Daddy, the guts came out.

After that, barbecues had to be moved to the driveway. Anytime you wanted to cut the grass you had to pat at the ground to scare the frogs away before you slowly moved the push-mower a foot or two. A whole afternoon spent carefully trimming the lawn made your short weekend even shorter.

You could often be found looking out the window longingly, the tall grass moving not because of the wind, but because of the frogs. They were bigger now, some of them dwarfing the kid's palms. Their dewy pale skin was now ridged and marked with dark stripes and spots. The kids were busy with swim camp and soccer camp. Your stay-cation now meant hours sitting on the sofa while your wife tried out new recipes from Vegetarian Times. Everyday when your children came home they asked you how Kermit-1 was doing. And Kermit-2, and Kermit-3, and so on.

And then the dog finally caught one. Then two. Then six. And then you both got a trip to the vet's office, where you wiped the never-ending stream of froth flowing from his canine lips gingerly as you waited. Perhaps they weren't all frogs, but some of them toads, the vet wondered. Thousands of dollars later you explained to the kids that you'd all have to wait out the night, hope that Ducky returned in the morning. And he did, but he couldn't go out back anymore. Instead, it was meandering walks down the street and short sniffs out by the wood chips on the west side of the house.

This is when you stopped sleeping. You'd lie awake at night, listening to the cree-cree, and the kuk kuk kuk, which replaced the noise machine your wife used to swear by. The sound reverberated in your head, frog legs beating on your eardrums in an inconsistent rhythm that reminded you that everything you do is a failure. The days were getting shorter. The cool mornings brought the promise of fall. The kids were trying on their back-to-school clothes. But the frogs were not going anywhere.

And that is why, you explain to the guy in the apron, you are looking at the end-of-season sale on riding lawnmowers for your measly 600 square foot backyard.

Lesley Alicia Tye *holds a BFA in Screenwriting from the University of Southern California, an MFA from National University, and teaches screenwriting and film in Michigan. She has a variety of credits in film and television, and received USC's Stephen C. Gentry Award for Excellence in Screenwriting. She blogs about screenwriting and can often be found roaming the woods with her toad-hunting mini-dachshund.*

BITE

Michael Crane

Martian

My love sometimes says to me, "You're off your planet," and she smiles and I wonder if she knows how much I adore her. In a world of fancy dancers, my love pirouettes around the truth for me to see through the lies of the world. She calls me her U.F.O. Her Unlimited Fun Object.

Every second of the day I try to come up with a game that will give her pleasure. Once, I got her to close her eyes and tell me how many stars were in the sky. She answered, "Twenty five thousand, six hundred and ninety seven." She squealed with delight when I told her she was correct, then she hugged me and asked how I knew. I shrugged my shoulders and replied, "I just know, that's all."

She loved it when I arranged for a meteor shower to parade in the sky for her birthday. She didn't ask me how I did this for it would take away the romance of my gift. Sometimes, she darts around the room like a comet wagging its tail to get me to pursue her. When we make love in her bedroom, I always leave the curtains wide open so that moonlight can bathe her naked body.

Sometimes, I recite poems to her in an ancient language and though she doesn't understand a word I'm saying she knows that I'm speaking from my heart the words that tell her I love her. Other times, we fight and she says things to hurt me. She has told me that I'm cold and that my heart is like a black hole sucking her into a dark chasm.

Last night we had a violent argument and I thought she was going to leave me forever. I knelt down in front of her and made my confession: "Maybe I'm not human, but an alien from another planet and I'm here to study what love is and you have taught me everything and now I must leave." She giggled to herself, and said, "Maybe I'm not from Earth either. Maybe I am a Martian, did you ever think of that?" My love took my hand, kissed me, and my heart imploded like the death of a million suns.

Michael Crane *has had more than 350 poems and stories published in literary journals in Australia and the US. He organizes the Poetry Idol Final for the Melbourne Writers Festival, is managing editor of the annual literary journal* The Paradise Anthology, *and performs musical poems and songs with Trish Anderson of acclaimed band* GIT.

BITE

James Bernard Frost

Agate

It was a hot day and we drove to the coast with her. It wasn't something we did often. She was beautiful and we adored her. She had long dark hair and olive skin and brown, wide-set eyes. She was Mom. We were playing music saved on our iPod. It was five guys from Australia who wore bright clothes in primary colors. Their jingles ran through our speakers. We sang along with them. We sang "Fruit salad, yummy, yummy."

She didn't sing.

We drove the station wagon up into the mountains that separated the coast from our town. We drove too fast and we didn't stay within lines. We were a Dad and two boys: sandy-haired, green-eyed, alike. We sang "Peel the banana, peel the banana." She said, "Why do you have to drive like that?" We knew but we couldn't explain.

We were going to a beach called Agate Beach. We'd agreed it was a good day to collect gems. The road was wiggly and so were we. We said, "When are we going to get there, Dad?" We said, "When are we going to get there, Donkey?" We snorted. Apple juice came out our nose. She glared at us. She said, "They'll choke on the straws." We were coming down off the mountains and we noticed how clear it was, how the fog wasn't there. We sang, "Take the knife. Take the knife."

We'd said *when are we going to get there, donkey* too many times. It wasn't funny anymore but we couldn't help ourselves. Finally, we said, "Look donkey we're here," and we were. Was agate blue? We didn't know. We knew the sky and ocean were blue and we imagined the agate would be as well. We popped the hatchback and took the shovels and buckets out. We were ready. There were gems to find.

She said, "You've forgotten the sunscreen."

And we had, we'd forgotten the sunscreen. She said, "He's only three." We looked at the sky and the sea and the dunes. We looked at our white skin. How could we explain? How could we say, let us burn? We tried, "But Mom." We argued, "The fog might roll in." We were back in the car. Five guys from Australia sang "slice the banana" but no one sang along.

We drove to the Wal-Mart. She asked us to drop her off in the front. We did this and then drove to the back of the parking lot. We saw fog coming up over eucalyptus trees. We said, "You're stinky." We said, "I'm

BITE

not stinky, you're stinky." We were doing it because we were bored. We said, "Mom's stinky." The fog enveloped the car. The Australians sang, "Mix it in a bowl." One of us said, "I am not stinky," and cried.

She came back with many plastic bags. There was a bright, striped umbrella wrapped in a plastic tube. There were sun hats. There was a loaf of bread and turkey and cheese and lettuce and tomatoes. There was soda water. There was sunscreen. She wasn't smiling. She said, "Why didn't you pick up the phone? How was I supposed to find you?" We looked at each other. We looked at the phone. Why hadn't we picked up the phone? We didn't know. Someone said, "Dad's stinky." We giggled. How could we explain?

We drove back to Agate Beach. Everything that was once blue was now gray. We unbuckled our seatbelts and opened our doors and ran. We couldn't be bothered. We couldn't be stopped. The buckets and shovels were left behind. There were dunes. We leapt off a dune and landed in sand. When we leapt, someone yelled "Cow!" While in the air, we replied "Moo!" We cowed and mooed from dune to dune.

One of us looked back and saw her. She was walking in a straight line. She had the many plastic bags and the multi-colored umbrella and the sun hats. She had a carpet too, which was dragging in the sand. Her hair was over her eyes and she was watching her feet. Someone leapt off a dune and yelled, "Heehaw!"

We found the first one at the bottom of a dune. "Agate," we said. We gathered round. It was small and cobalt, flat on both sides. We didn't have the buckets so we cupped it in our hands. "Let's find more," we said. We spread out and hunted. There was agate everywhere on Agate Beach. It was blue and green and yellow and orange, thin and flat and jagged on the sides. Primary and secondary colors. We cupped the agate in our hands. We said, "Look at this one!" and did. We went up and down the dunes and made sure we knew where we were. We were little and didn't want to lose each other.

We did this for a while. We did this 'til our hands were full. We came together and examined the gems. "Let's sell them," we said. "No," we said, "let's give them to Mom."

We had a hard time finding her. The fog was thick. We followed the sound of the waves and made our way towards the water. One of us was tired and needed to be carried. The agate seemed heavy now, not worth as much. There was a stiff breeze. We saw the multi-colored umbrella first, blurry in the sea haze. The older one ran. The Dad walked with the younger one on his shoulder and the gems in his hands. How could he explain?

When we arrived, we laid them on the carpet at her feet. We were proud. "Agate," we said. She looked at the gems then looked at us. We were covered in sand. We had sand in our pants and our shoes and our ears. We had sand in our eyes and it hurt. She squinted at us. "He's sunburned," she said.

We looked. It was hard to tell. Were we sunburned?

She looked at the pile of agate. "It's plastic," she said. "Little plastic chips. Cups and toys and things ground up in the surf. Phytoestrogens get released into the ocean. They kill life. There are dead zones."

She had these eyes, these dark downturned eyes. She looked like she was alone, like she wasn't with us at all.

She said, "It's cold here."

We hadn't noticed it was cold before.

We shivered.

We knew when she walked the dunes we'd lose her forever.

James Bernard Frost *is the author of* A Very Minor Prophet *(Hawthorne Books),* World Leader Pretend, *and the award-winning travel guide* The Artichoke Trail. *His writing has been published in the* San Francisco Examiner, *the* San Francisco Bay Guardian, *and* Wired. *He lives in Portland, Oregon with the author Kerry Cohen, their four children, the rain, the freaks, and the trees. His bike is currently in disrepair.*

Mary Emerick

Freezeout Road

Our neighbor never left his house on Freezeout Road. His Subaru sported expired tags. All we saw of him was a ten-foot fence shutting us out and the coyote carcasses piercing his gate. I told Iris that something wasn't right there. Iris said that nobody moved to Freezeout Road because they were normal. She looked at me as she said it, and I knew she was still waiting on a ring. A normal guy would have proposed to her by now, she was probably thinking. She had invested most of her thirties already. She had said it all before.

She was right, though. On Freezeout Road, we were all waiting for life to happen to us. Except for Iris. She bullied life until it gave in to her. She had bullied her way into my house, a force of nature impossible to fight. Why she stuck around, I didn't know, except that Iris loved projects.

"Maybe the fence is so elk don't get into his garden," Iris told me one day after her walk. She made a note on her Gary list: Build a fence. The lumber sat under a tarp. I was going to get to it. "Or maybe he's a reclusive millionaire," she said. "Or a movie star."

In summertime, she walked by that house every day wearing a sundress, her big shoulders white and freckled. She wanted something to happen. Nothing ever happened on Freezeout Road, but she made up stories sometimes. She saw a wolf. She ran out of water and nearly died. I usually turned up the radio when she started in on her stories.

"The whole world forgets about you after the turn off the county road," Iris said once. She was right about that, too. Freezeout Road was a rattlesnake, twisting deep into the heart of the scorched yellow mountain. Driving up the ruts, I felt swallowed, the rest of the world just something I had dreamed up.

It was hot on Freezeout Road, the kind of hot where you don't want to do a damn thing. Iris came back from her walk tomato-faced and wheezing. I sat on the porch. The supports needed shoring up.

"He tried to pull me in his car," she hollered.

I looked at her broad arms and back and raised my eyebrows. It was hard to imagine.

"For the love of god," she said, going to call the cops.

After the feds showed up and took him, the news went around Freezeout Road that he was an escaped

BITE

felon, wanted for kidnapping and murder years ago in another state. Iris squealed. "I could have been his next victim," she said. "I would have died a single woman. Childless." She was winding up.

To escape, I took a walk up Freezeout Road. I knew the end of my freedom was near. There was no way out. The heat made it hard to even think about winter. It would always be this hot, our lives always the same.

At the felon's gate, the coyotes had shriveled up to nothing. If I looked just right, Iris hung there instead, her long dirt-colored hair waving in the wind, her mouth forever stilled.

Mary Emerick *has supported her writing habit over the years by working in various occupations including wildland firefighter, kayak ranger, and tree planter. Her essays have appeared in several anthologies and magazines. In 2012, she was a Pushcart Prize nominee and a finalist for the* High Desert Journal's *Obsidian Prize. She lives in Joseph, Oregon, and blogs at http://mountainsskin.blogspot. com.*

Tara L. Masih

Fire-on-the-Water

I surprised my father tonight. The whole town of Monterosso, in fact.

We have lived by the Ligurian Sea for so long, we eat it, absorb it, breathe it. As children, we grew up with stories of how the sea saved us from Those Barbarians who were afraid of its power and would not venture down the sea cliffs. We were saved by the sea, over and over, in our history and in our bedtime stories.

But tonight, it turns on us. The incessant rains have pushed the water over the rivers' banks, flooding our seaside towns. And from the other side, the rough seas rage against the protective sea walls and the pebble beaches. The siren began an hour ago. I look out from behind the shutter to see our old fishermen trying to save their *lamparas,* stored on the coarse shingle for the usually mild winter.

My mother likes to say my father's eyes match the color of the sea because of generations spent fishing and swimming in them. When I was young, he used to take me out at night in his wooden spotlight boat. We'd row along the sea beds, the lamps torching out over the black water to find the fire-on-the-water, the green glow of luminescent plankton that draws in the "bread of the sea," the anchovies. But I did not want to be there. I did not have the patience to sit in that glow for hours, waiting for the sea to churn to a gray froth of fish, to haul them all in with the old, knotted, spiky nets. It was long, dull, painful work, and when we pulled into the beach to meet my mother, waiting with her terracotta pots to gather them, the haul seemed paltry and meager and not worth the time.

Most of us in town grew up with the smell of the smoke house sheds doing their work in the backyards, and with the smell of brine and fresh fish in the house as mothers gutted and scaled and stuffed the red, inner flesh. We helped them gather the scales' pearlessence so it could be trucked off and ground into lipstick and fake pearls and God knows what else. We watched them walk the *sentiri* trails along the sea cliffs to the neighboring villages to trade. And we knew we would not be making this same trek. We took our bikes and cars up the mountain and away, down the flat highways to the cities.

But now, I see a blue *lampara* disappear under a wave almost tidal in proportion, and when the wave drags back, the boat is gone. And I hear the dim cries go up from the crowd below. Muffled wails of such despair. The sea has turned on us in the past, but never like this, not with so much power and ability to take all.

I run out of the cliff house and down the slippery stone stairs to the main town road, cross the playground, and fight my way against the rain and wind, pushing to get to the others. It is like a wall of resistance I have to break through. The siren continues to call out. When I reach the beach, I see my friend Carlo already there, and Vanni, the son of the cheesemaker. I join in the fight to save the colorful boats that our ancestors built and mended with such respect. As the sea tries to take one from me, I groan and bleed and fight to hold on, fall on my side. Looking up, I see my father crawling against heavy currents to reach me, and I catch a shimmery gray glint of something about to overflow from his eyes.

For Her Sixtieth Birthday in Cambridge, Massachusetts

It was as if they had arrived for her sixtieth birthday. The day after, in fact, when she was taking out her garbage to the aluminum can in the alley. A pair of bright yellow birds in the Mimosa tree that hung from her neighbor's yard over the broken asphalt area. Some kind of parakeet, she surmised, watching them flutter and hop branch to branch, like they were testing out each one. These birds didn't belong. She knew someone must have released them. Maybe together, or maybe they had found each other. Like the feral parrots in San Francisco she'd heard about on TV. But that was a warm city. She had never seen parrots in the wild in frigid New England, and in the city, no less.

She took to bringing out from her apartment a

blue vinyl folding chair that used to travel with her to Crane's Beach, back when the kids were around, the latticework seating now brittle and frayed. She sat beneath the tree branches, eating her liverwurst on decrusted dark rye, watching, listening. They were there to teach her something. She listened to their chirps and songs. She bought canary bird seed at the local hardware store and sprinkled it on top of the landlord's rusty green dumpster for them to forage on. She worried about winter when the tree's silky pink flowers quickly turned brown, a reminder of how temporal it all was. She wondered how anyone could abandon anything so lovely and tragically vulnerable.

The following week, on garbage day, when she shuffled into the alleyway with her plastic bag, they'd vanished. Still, she unfolded her aluminum chair every summer afternoon, beside her plaid thermos, ate her sandwich, and stared into the empty umbrella-like overhang. She tried to remember what freedom looked like.

Tara L. Masih *is editor of* The Rose Metal Press Field Guide to Writing Flash Fiction *(a ForeWord Book of the Year) and author of* Where the Dog Star Never Glows *(a National Best Books Award finalist). Awards for her work include first place in* The Ledge Magazine*'s fiction contest and Pushcart Prize,* Best New American Voices, *and Best of the Web nominations.*

Bruce Holland Rogers
Riding with Icarus

Richardson has been reading Bullfinch's mythology lately. He'd been meaning to get to it for years. The book followed him from college, one apartment to the next. He'd had the book through two jobs, a return to school for his MBA, a failed marriage, promotions, a better marriage, fatherhood, even better promotions and moves from this house to that one to yet another. Only now, after his retirement, after his wife has died, after his first heart surgery, is he actually starting to read.

And reading, he has found himself among the immortals. For instance, his golfing partner, Taylor, has a bad day of shanks or long drives straight into the water. By the twelfth green, Taylor's face is red, and he shakes his putter with menace. Periphetes, Richardson thinks. Periphetes and his iron club.

When Richardson gets his prescriptions filled, he notices the dark, scheming gaze of the pharmacist, and he recognizes her. Here is Medea, taking a job where she has ready access to potions.

And then there is his grandson. Richardson needs someone to drive him to and from the hospital for tests and procedures, and his daughter-in-law volunteers Luke for the job. Luke isn't happy. To show it, he rides the bumpers of other cars. He corners fast. He punches the accelerator for yellow lights. Apparently he had other plans for the day, even though his mother had imagined a wide-open schedule.

The trip home from the doctor two hours later is the same. Tires squeal. Luke propels the car in lurches between lanes to grab another ten feet of advantage over other drivers. You're going to get us killed, son, Richardson thinks of saying. But doesn't. Just then, he knows his grandson, and he knows that there's no telling him anything. The boy has never listened, not in thousands of years.

They are traveling west, into the late afternoon glare.

"Faster," Richardson says. "Come on, let's open 'er up. Let's see what this baby can do!"

His grandson grins. There is no happiness like his. He laughs. They are both laughing. "All right," the boy says, and aims the car into the sun. "Here we go!"

BITE

Bruce Holland Rogers *lives in Eugene, Oregon, the tie-dye capital of the world. For six years, Bruce wrote a column about the spiritual and psychological challenges of full-time fiction writing for* Speculations *magazine. Many of those columns have been collected in a book,* Word Work: Surviving and Thriving as a Writer. *He is currently a member of the permanent faculty at the Whidbey Writers Workshop MFA program and publishes his own short-short stories by e-mail through www.short shortshort.com.*

Caleb True

Shop-Vac

The teacher said "Don't use dreams as a plot device, it is too typical"—well Hey, guess what, in my dreams there really is a man who pulls down his pants and instead of a, you know, he's got a Shop-Vac hose, and it's turned on, waving around and sucking and sucking and it's pulling at my shirt until it comes off, and I'm in my bra, and the man laughs and chases after me, so what am I supposed to do? The man chases me all through the house and his Vac thing is sucking up dust bunnies and quarters and jewelry, getting stuck in the carpeting, and he trips over it and swears, and I'm looking back and trying to stay ahead of him, thinking how to get out of there without getting sucked and then he corners me in the kitchen. I back into the basement door and open it, and he chases after me, clomp clomp clomp, down the steps into the dusty cement darkness, and I head for the breaker box, but he has my hair in his Vac, pulling it out in strands. I tear my hair away and open the breaker box, switch all the switches off, and all around me in the big house things are powering down with small mournful sounds, and the Vac Man is swearing and saying "No, No," and I don't know what I've done, but he is on the floor and his thing isn't vacuuming anymore and then he looks up and says, "Please, I'll die!" (and No, fyi, he's not my father; it's not a Freudian thing). He wants me to turn his power back on, so I say, "Where's my shirt?" realizing how chilly it is down there. He points a shaking finger at the corner of the basement, where a key ring dangles from a nail. I go and fetch it, and I plug the key right into the man's back, and open him up. "Inside," he says, and liquid pours out of his back, his guts are all there, pumping and burbling. I reach in and feel around, squeezing and pushing, palpitating and fingering for fabric. "Hurry, please," gasps the Vac Man, expiring there on the concrete floor. I find it near the front of his body, tucked in next to his liver—How did it get there?—and then I close him back up, hang my shirt over a pipe to drip dry, and go to the breaker box to restore power. I flip the switch, and his hose starts sucking again, but that's it. He's gone already, his thing sucking away at the cold basement air, and I won't be able to write about it for anyone.

BITE

Caleb True *writes stories. He lives in New England. He holds an MA in History from University of Massachusetts. His favorite food is Pad Kee Mao. His fiction can be found either right now or in the future in* The Portland Review, Moon City Review, *and elsewhere.*

Alex Mindt

Burning Woman

Above me, the head of a bull, paper maché, blue and orange and oranger, and then orange and red, and then no bull, just teeth, small, human teeth, white in the dark night under fists clenched above shaved heads and ratty heads, dreadlocked heads, and music, or sounds that sounded like music coming from some distant darkness.

Star, his name was, or that's what he said his name was, or the name he'd given himself, years after his parents had burdened him with Adam or Ken, and now, alone, at 19 years old, with his hand on my breast, proclaiming that god exists in the tongues of the fire, in the capillaries in the tips of his fingers. "Even though there is no god, but the god we imagine."

He was lost, a lost genius, dropped out of college as a senior at 19, disillusioned, he said, by information and its discontents, by "intellectual vanity." "There is more truth in a s single stone out here," he said, pointing around at the large egg-shaped rocks that lay on the desert floor around us, "than any philosophical theory, than any scientific proof. There's more truth in a lie than there is in fact. Fact!" he shouted.

He had a hairlip, scar tissue bumped and jagged running down the valley of his philtrum, which rounded his r's into curious growls. And I probably shouldn't say this but his fingers on my breast did for a second remind me that the darkness around us was all that we had, and his earnest, funny voice that said love too easily and said touch my stones, touch the fruit of my stones, whatever that meant, whatever anything meant, just that my skin loved everything, touch meant eternity, and I was thirsty, so thirsty I couldn't stop opening and closing my mouth. I wanted the breeze to keep blowing on my skin. Was I naked? Partly, I think. "Nude!" Star said. "An artist's rendition. Naked is too crass for you!" We were dancing around a fire, the music mechanical, or technical, like computers, and buzzing and beeping with the solid thumping that shook the ground under my feet and his other hand on my other breast and people around us not even looking and me not caring and I think about it now and wonder who was that person, and how did she end up there? Older and fatter than every unshowered neo-hippy around me, dancing in a bra and tan Bermuda shorts, bare feet, hips unhinged, not even attached to my fat, old body, my eyes

BITE

closed with fingers from this short, nerdy boy, tracing the loneliest places, remembering that once people thought I was pretty, me, pretty.

Did he want to know what happened? Did anyone ask why this Target-shopping, middle-aged, size 14 suburban mom was out here, alone, in the middle of nowhere, floating somewhere in the firelight, after swallowing a single pill she'd not ever, not once in her life, ever thought about, or ever even had the chance to take. But what do you tell these kids even if they do ask? Do you tell them about the boxes you went through in your dead mother's closet? About the things you found—her list, her long list of regrets?

Wipeout

My father hasn't come by in a while. He used to come over a lot. Mom would take him into the kitchen to talk to him before he'd come to my room and say, "Sandra? Ready to go?"

Usually we'd go to the dog park and sit on a picnic table and watch the dogs fetch balls and run in and out of the muddy slough with sticks in their mouths. Sometimes we'd talk about things like what dog we might steal if we had the guts, and sometimes we wouldn't talk at all, but just sit there and watch.

In the winter we'd go to the Starship Cinemas and sneak from theater to theater, seeing every movie until they closed. If a movie had a dog in it, especially a talking dog, or a dog whose thoughts we could hear, we'd just sit there and watch that movie over and over, applauding at the end every time.

But surfer movies were his favorite. Anything with surfing, he loved. I don't know why. He'd never even been to the ocean.

My father lived in a house that smelled like dirty laundry, a big house with lots of bedrooms but only two bathrooms and one kitchen that everyone shared. The other men in there were like my father. Something had gone wrong with them, and they were recovering. My dad had been recovering for ten years. Mom said he'd never get any better.

When I was five, he and his best friend Marty were roofing Marty's parent's house. It was a hot summer day and they were drinking beer, a lot of beer, my mom says. Somehow, my father tripped and fell two stories onto the concrete steps below.

I remember going to the hospital and visiting him as he lay there with a cast on his arm and a blank stare on his face. He couldn't talk for a long time and then words started coming out one by one. He slurred like he was drunk. But over time he got better. Now he talks, but he thinks a lot and then speaks slowly, with a little bit of space between each word.

After I entered high school, the trips to the movies and the dog park happened less and less. Playing in the marching band, running on the cross-country team and stage-managing the spring musical took up all of my time. Talking to my father about surfing and dogs, and how cool it would be to see a talking-dog surf movie just wasn't going to happen.

Sometimes he'd show up at the football games, and he'd clap and shout my name so loud, I swear he embarrassed even strangers. When people asked me who he was, I told them he was my uncle.

A few months ago, I asked him to stop coming to the games. It was the hardest thing I'd ever done.

He sat across from me at the kitchen table. Mom was leaning against the counter, sipping her coffee. He was quiet. I had grown used to his silence, but it still made Mom uncomfortable.

"Is everything okay, David?" she said, as if she were talking to a child.

"I like music," he said, and then he tried to smile. "I'm just glad you are playing an instrument."

"I can play it for you," I said. "It's just that at the games, it's kind of strange."

"She doesn't even want me there," Mom said.

Tears filled his eyes, and I knew I had done something wrong, something irreparable and foolish.

"I'd like to hear you play," he said, wiping his eyes.

"Okay," I said. "I'll practice a song and then I'll play it for you, all right? The theme from *Hawaii Five O*, or how about *Wipeout?*"

Alex Mindt *somehow got an MFA in Fiction at Columbia University. He has published numerous short stories and poems, and his book* Male of the Species *was a finalist for the Pen/Bingham Award and the William Saroyan Prize. He has written and directed two feature films—* Nowheresville *and* OxyContin Blues—*and for a while he made a living counting cards in Las Vegas. He currently teaches at Adelphi University.*

BITE

Sherrie Flick

Microwave

She put the dog in the microwave for 22 seconds. Or she dreamed she put the dog in the microwave for 22 seconds. The dog, nonetheless, spun on the little plate and howled mercilessly for 10 seconds and then lay down and spun silently for the last part. Susan didn't know which was worse—the howling or the silence. And she doesn't know why she put the dog in the microwave, as instructed. It seemed important at the time though. Whether Susan dreamed it or not seemed irrelevant, because it seemed she should be able to make ethical decisions even while dreaming.

It was important to put the dog in the microwave, part of a process that helped the dog, but she knew it wasn't true even as she pushed the button. Was that her mother's microwave? The one mounted above the stove? The dog didn't like heights either so that made it awful in a two-fold way.

The dog, backlit, spun like a carnival ride. The howling was like mourning, like crying for real.

She woke before she could open the microwave door—pressing the thick plastic button so the door would pop free to expose her smoking puppy. She awoke and her real dog—a small Yorkshire terrier that would, in fact, fit into a microwave with little problem, was sleeping, curled up beside her. His back nestled against her own—trusting, in love. A little dog lover, sleeping but waking as soon as she did, ready for the day. Tail wagging. Happy, really.

The dog would've smoked and then, stood up. Better? Perhaps he would've been improved in the dream. Was it a means to get rid of fleas? Was that the idea?

Susan pet the dog who rolled on his back, exposing his belly with a white tuft of hair. Crazy happy. Crazy in love. The dog would lie like that for a very long time as she lightly stroked his hair, curls sprouting along his tiny feet.

Susan knew she needed to stop this kind of dreaming. Damning dreams, night after night. She pulled her robe closer and descended the creaking stairs, her feet tender from yesterday's hike. Her hip joints reluctant to move again so soon. The dog scampered ahead of her, sure of the routine. Susan opened the door to a bright fall day. Breezes and the windchimes tinkling. The dog raced into the yard while she watched, admiringly. He was a handsome dog, a good dog nearly all the time.

BITE

Except around babies where he would yap and nip with jealousy and Susan would scream at him, embarrassing herself and her friends.

The dog scampered back inside without incident, and Susan got to work in the kitchen: espresso, newspaper, granola with milk and bananas. Nothing seemed amiss except for that lingering idea of the dog spinning slowly on the glass plate, the interior of the oven smelling of tomato sauce, of reheated pizza.

Susan had separated from Peter a month before. She'd asked him late at night as they lay side by side in bed, the dog stretched between them as a buffer. She'd asked him nicely, had practiced, actually into a mirror beforehand. Even though his eyes had been closed for the delivery, she'd read somewhere, though, that facial expressions affect inflection.

She'd told him she needed time, and it was true. She needed to be alone. Peter seemed exhausted when he agreed to it, like what next. That was his position right now on the world: What next? He just took it, like a casual pass of the ball, and trotted out and moved in with his friend, Billy.

Alone, Susan walked the house looking at their things. All the things they'd acquired over the years. Rocks from hikes and books—so many books about nature and gardening and literature old and new. There were the lace curtains she'd insisted upon. Soon, it seemed like her house; she understood this. It had always been her house, and Peter had just lived in it. He could walk away that easily, start anew. Whatever she wanted, really, he was okay with that. But that was exactly what she didn't want. She wanted someone to fight for her. And why, she wondered didn't the dog fight? When she'd set it into the microwave, it had sat primly, happy, its tongue partway out, smiling like dogs do. Then she'd pressed the button—and only when it couldn't be helped (Why couldn't it be helped? She could've pressed the big black button earlier, yes?) did it howl and give up.

Susan wanted a different world. It's true. She wanted to have the dog in her arms, to hear the request, to shake her head no. To walk out, away, into a sunset.

Sherrie Flick *is the author of the flash fiction chapbook* I Call This Flirting *(Flume) and the novel* Reconsidering Happiness *(Bison Books). She lives in Pittsburgh, where she writes and teaches and edits and gardens and cooks.*

BITE

Andrew Kozma

The Beast

I can see it from the plane's window, the beast's bulk a wart on the horizon. The top of the beast crests through the clouds. Even from this distance—the pilot claims we're a hundred miles away—I can see texture on the side of the beast, thick, ropy columns like the head of a mop prepared to scrub the landscape clean. All color at this distance is grey, but I imagine the beast green. A bright green like that of a B-movie Martian. Below the clouds, below the body of the beast, is Cleveland.

Was Cleveland.

The plane from Detroit to Houston is full, as is every plane out of Detroit these days. There is plenty of time to evacuate. Even in the midst of this crisis, moving companies are making a killing. The guys I hired are charging four thousand dollars. They will pack up my apartment and send everything along after me, packed tightly into an eighteen-wheeler that will navigate roads already thick with cars.

I picture the cars on the road as spawning salmon. All the footage I've seen shows cars stuck on shoulders and angled into ditches, though the news doesn't dwell on it. They don't want to cause a panic. They don't want another roadside shootout. They don't want another highway robbery. They don't want people riding shotgun with shotguns.

Riding on the plane with us are six federal marshals. They try to be unobtrusive. They stay where they were when we entered. Two are outside the cabin, one is in the rear, and the other three have aisle seats evenly spaced throughout the length of the plane. They keep their feet out of the aisle. They are careful with their elbows.

The beast moves slowly. Scientists have measured its speed at a mile a day. There are people left in Cleveland who refused to abandon their homes. I understand why. Yes, the beast is several miles high. Yes, the government has issued warnings.

But when a fear is part of your life day in and day out, you cease to be afraid. The beast is part of your skyline for weeks, for months. You wake up in the morning and its presence is comforting. You come to believe that the beast was meant to be there. That its role in your life will never change. That you don't want it to change.

And then one day you find the beast has eaten

BITE

the school and the corner store, the YMCA and the library. The power has been down for days, but your generator is still running. From the fridge, you grab a beer. You grab a tub of tuna salad and a tomato. You grab a knife.

On the porch, you watch it approach. The beer is crisp and tastes of earth. You slice the tomato and eat those slices with dollops of tuna salad. From this distance, you can see the beast move, each column of flesh rippling forward individually. It is late afternoon and the sun is shining directly on the flesh of the beast. It glimmers in the light like a mirage.

Andrew Kozma's *stories have appeared or will appear in* NANO Fiction, Front Range Review, and DIAGRAM. *His first book of poems,* City of Regret *(Zone 3 Press, 2007), won the Zone 3 First Book Award. His chapbook,* A Natural History, *written with Michelle Schmidt, was published by Blue Hour Press.*

Ester Bloom

The Sex Lives of Other People

"People don't save people, Annie," he says.

It's the morning after and he's talking to me like Caesar Milan, gentle but firm. I hate that. Also the side-part in his hair, the way he burps, his under-tipping at restaurants (and nothing for baristas, as though his coffee simply materializes, like a genie, because he rubbed two coins together). "Who's asking anyone to save anyone?" I say, standing on his doorstep.

Last night I showed up on this doorstep, panties in my purse, risking my pride because I knew that anyone could have been up there with him: a student, his ex-wife, a genie or an ingénue, two underwear models and a euphonium, my god, a whole marching band in various states of undress, I wouldn't be surprised. I like that he likes sex. I'm not sentimental about who he has it with. But nobody likes to be *de trop*. He buzzed me in, and we spent the night focusing on the good parts about him (he keeps robes in his bathroom for guests; he is generous with alcohol and compliments; he knows how to use his hands; I love him, or he was the last man I loved—more or less the same thing).

Now, he's being cryptic. A few drops of real sadness dilute his voice, and fat drops of rain hit my hair, still wet from his shower. I didn't bring an umbrella. My sister says it is one of my cardinal faults that I never think far enough ahead to bring umbrellas or make reservations or fuck the sort of person I could grow old with. "You need to have your own life," he says. "You need to save yourself. That's how it works in the real world."

It takes effort not to roll my eyes. This man might not be rich-rich, but he's rich enough, richer than I am, and I do all right. He sleeps on Egyptian cotton. He has someone else do his laundry. He buys art. Before I can reply, or step forward into the dryness of the vestibule to have this conversation, he flaps his hand in the air between us.

"I'm sorry," he says. "Forget it."

"No, it's okay." I always say that when I mean the opposite. "But you should be honest with yourself. You want to save somebody—everybody does."

"Annie."

"No, really. I'm not the right lady for you. Fine. But don't pretend you don't want to be somebody's hero."

BITE

"I really don't," says Alex.

"All right," I say, shrugging. He's lying to both of us. My eyes burn with indignation but tears would be a third kind of wet, and who needs it. We're only having this conversation now because I had a weepy moment when I woke up, and he asked me what was wrong, and, without thinking, I told him about the divorce. He acted sympathetic in the moment but I know his discomfort is what's behind this scene in the doorway. If ordinary people have the 36-crayon Crayola box of emotions, he only has the most basic eight-color set; more complicated blends of feelings are beyond his comprehension.

I turn to leave. Alex says, "Here." He grabs me an umbrella from the stand, tall enough to be a cane, its skin deep violet, its handle slick and tan. For a second I almost laugh, because he is handing me some other cast-off woman's cast-off umbrella, and he doesn't seem to see the irony—his face shows only the single serving of sympathy he has allotted me. His hairline has inched back and his nose forward since we met. Men get older too, though I forget that sometimes. His nose has heft to it, substance; it's more mountain than hill.

"I'll call you," he says.

I'll miss his nose. I think of leaving the umbrella, but that won't help the previous cast-off and it won't help me. Instead I open up my own small violet sky and hold tight to the fake-wood handle and walk away.

Ester Bloom's *writing has appeared in* Salon, The Hairpin, The Awl, Nerve, The Morning News, PANK, Bluestem, Phoebe, Zone 3, *and* Creative Nonfiction, *among other venues. She blogs on culture for* The Huffington Post *and is a columnist for* Cheek Teeth Blog *and* The Billfold. *Her collection of essays,* Never Marry a Short Woman, *is represented by Michele Rubin at Writers House.*

BITE

Tom Weller

Hercules Massis

The men have come to hear the snap of a jawbone, to see teeth shatter, gums explode, blood blooming in the air like fireworks. They clap their oil-stained hands, stomp their boots in the gravel lining the tracks. They buy bags of popcorn from a strolling vendor. They yell, "Give 'em hell." They yell, "You can do it, Mate." They pretend they have come to root for Hercules Massis.

They have come to root for the train.

Hercules Massis waves to the men. He flexes his arms, pounds his chest, a sound like a bass drum. He waves again and smiles, shows off his mighty choppers. He pretends the men have come to root for him. He pretends he doesn't feel profoundly alone.

Hercules takes the bit in his mouth. The metal

feels warm against his lips, tastes electric on his tongue. He takes a deep breath, stares down his challenge. An eight-foot length of rope, thick around as a baseball bat, connects the bit in his mouth to the train, one locomotive and two box cars.

The men grow impatient, their shouts more insistent. "Come on. Let's go." Several complain about the heat of the day. Pigeons scramble among their feet scavenging dropped popcorn. Hercules closes his eyes, hears only his own voice in his head chanting: "Her. Cue. Lees. Her. Cue. Lees." His heartbeat slows. Hercules is ready.

A man wearing a bowler hat fires a starter pistol. Pigeons burst into the air. Hercules Massis takes one easy step backward. The rope goes taut. Silence.

Through squinted eyes Hercules sees the nose of the locomotive. Blood pounds in his ears. Veins and tendons bulge, furrow the skin of his neck and shoulders. He feels all the weight of the train in his mouth.

The nose of the locomotive is shiny and silver, rounded and sleek. Hercules wants to touch it, to feel its curves warm against his palm. He reaches back with one foot, braces the sole of his boot against the railroad tie. Strains. Nothing. Not even a millimeter. He hears his own voice in his head: "Her. Cue. Lees. Her. Cue. Lees."

The men grow loud. They yell, "Come on, come on." They yell, "You can do it."

Hercules hears a hundred voices yelling, "Break his mouth. Break him." His chest becomes hollow. Lead fills his stomach. Still he strains, against the weight of

BITE

the train, against the hopes of the men. Hercules wants to lie down and cry.

He feels it first in his ankle. The completion of a tiny backward step. Movement. He hears it first in the change in the men's voices. The tone rises, the words jumble: "Did you see. Oh my God. Can't be. No." Hercules strains again. Boot heel pushes against railroad tie. A subtle rotation of steel wheels, and Hercules hears the train calling to him. Its voice, high-pitched and pretty as birdsong, drowns out the noise of the men. The train says, "I'm coming to you, Hercules. I'm coming." And Hercules reaches back with his foot again. Another backward step, bigger, easier than before. Momentum. And at that moment, the lead in Hercules's stomach becomes three hundred butterflies, and his hollow chest fills with helium. For the first time in his life Hercules Massis is in love. He wants to run to the train and stroke it, whisper promises and thanks to it. But he knows he must wait. There will be time for that later, away from the crowd. For now, they must dance, Hercules leading, the train following, moving together to a chorus of disappointed men's voices mumbling conjecture about fakery.

Tomorrow morning the newspapers will proclaim, *Hercules Massis, Man with the World's Strongest Teeth.* They will trumpet the numbers: 140 tons pulled over 10 meters. But Hercules Massis will remember most clearly the sound that train made as it rolled down the track, "Her. Cue. Lees. Her. Cue. Lees," calling to him, insistent, uninhibited, the way lovers do, and the way a bit in the mouth can feel just like a kiss.

Tom Weller *is a former factory worker, Peace Corps volunteer, and Planned Parenthood sexuality educator. He currently lives in Greencastle, Indiana, and teaches at Indiana State University. His fiction and creative nonfiction have appeared recently in* Trachodon, Booth, Evening Street Review, Midwestern Gothic, *and the anthology* One Hand Does Not Catch a Buffalo: Fifty Years of Amazing Peace Corps Stories.

BITE

About the Editors

Katey Schultz *grew up in Portland, Oregon and is most recently from Celo, North Carolina. She is the editor of two fiction anthologies,* Dots on a Map *and* Coming Home *(Main Street Rag), and has contributed to the editorial staffs of six different literary magazines. Her flash fiction has received awards or recognition from River Styx, Whispering Prairie Press, Fish Publishing, Greensboro Writers of the Triad, and more. Her first book,* Flashes of War, *will be published May 2013 by Loyola University Maryland's Apprentice House Press. Learn more at www.kateyschultz.com.*

John Carr Walker *grew up on a raisin farm in California's San Joaquin Valley and now lives in Saint Helens, Oregon, where there's not a vineyard for miles. He's the editor of TRACHODON Magazine, the founder of Trachodon Publishing LLC, and was a Summer Fishtrap Fellow in 2012. His short fiction has appeared in* StringTown, Slow Trains, Prick of the Spindle, Prime Number, Eclectica, *and elsewhere. His short story collection* Repairable Men *is forthcoming from Sunnyoutside. He's currently finishing a novel dealing with the relationship between a family of migrant workers and a Japanese-American family during World War II in rural central California.*

The Grove Review
Summer 2012
Issue 6

Featuring fresh talent from
across the country in poetry,
short fiction, and art.

Interviews with translator and
editor Greg Simon and 2010
Walt Whitman Award winner
Carl Adamshick

BITE